TLDR CLASSICS
Frankenstein,
or the modern Prometheus

Mary Wollstonecraft (Godwin) Shelley

D1738538

ISBN:
978-1481255233

LIQUID HELIUM

This book is abridged from the original work by Mary Shelly. But it was not abridged by a human, instead it was automatically reduced using Stremor's advance language heuristics engine, Liquid Helium. We did this as an interesting experiment to challenge our technology's ability to analyze language and reduce the length of content.

Abridging fiction is much more challenging than working with non-fiction, and as you will find when reading this book, working with 100 year old English is much more difficult than the English of today. Despite these challenges we think you will find this short version of this classic work enjoyable, and we are very proud of the result.

For more information about Stremor and Liquid Helium, just visit http://www.stremor.com.

Liquid Helium: read less, grok more.

.

How slowly the time passes here, encompassed as I am by frost and snow! Yet a second step is taken towards my enterprise.

I desire the company of a man who could sympathize with me, whose eyes would reply to mine. You may deem me romantic, my dear sister, but I bitterly feel the want of a friend. How would such a friend repair the faults of your poor brother! Now I am twenty-eight and am in reality more illiterate than many schoolboys of fifteen. Yet some feelings, unallied to the dross of human nature, beat even in these rugged bosoms. My lieutenant, for instance, is a man of wonderful courage and enterprise; he is madly desirous of glory, or rather, to word my phrase more characteristically, of advancement in his profession. The master is a person of an excellent disposition and is remarkable in the ship for his gentleness and the mildness of his discipline. I heard of him first in rather a romantic manner, from a lady who owes to him the happiness of her life. This, briefly, is his story. My generous friend reassured the suppliant, and on being informed of the name of her lover, instantly abandoned his pursuit. He had already bought a farm with his money, on which he had designed to pass the remainder of his life; but he bestowed the whole on his rival, together with the remains of his prize-money to purchase stock, and then himself solicited the young woman's father to consent to her marriage with her lover. But the old man decidedly refused, thinking himself bound in honour to my friend, who, when he found the father inexorable, quitted his country, nor returned until he heard that his former mistress was married according to her inclinations. "What a noble fellow!" you will exclaim.

Yet do not suppose, because I complain a little or because I can conceive a consolation for my toils which I may never know, that I am wavering in my resolutions.

I cannot describe to you my sensations on the near prospect of my undertaking. There is something at work in my soul which I do not understand. I love you very tenderly. Remember me with affection, should you never hear from me again.

Adieu, my dear Margaret. I will be cool, persevering, and prudent.

But success SHALL crown my endeavours.

My swelling heart involuntarily pours itself out thus. But I must finish. Heaven bless my beloved sister!

Last Monday (July 31st) we were nearly surrounded by ice, which closed in the ship on all sides, scarcely leaving her the sea-room in which she floated.

I profited of this time to rest for a few hours.

On perceiving me, the stranger addressed me in English, although with a foreign accent.

Margaret, if you had seen the man who thus capitulated for his safety, your surprise would have been boundless. His limbs were nearly frozen, and his body dreadfully emaciated by fatigue and suffering. I never saw a man in so wretched a condition.

"Then I fancy we have seen him, for the day before we picked you up we saw some dogs drawing a sledge, with a man in it, across the ice."

"And yet you rescued me from a strange and perilous situation; you have benevolently restored me to life."

From this time a new spirit of life animated the decaying frame of the stranger.

The stranger has gradually improved in health but is very silent and appears uneasy when anyone except myself enters his cabin. Yet his manners are so conciliating and gentle that the sailors are all interested in him, although they have had very little communication with him. For my own part, I begin to love him as a brother, and his constant and deep grief fills me with sympathy and compassion. I said in one of my letters, my dear Margaret, that I should find no friend on the wide ocean; yet I have found a man who, before his spirit had been broken by misery, I should have been happy to have possessed as the brother of my heart.

My affection for my guest increases every day. As I spoke, a dark gloom spread over my listener's countenance.

You would not if you saw him.

You may easily imagine that I was much gratified by the offered communication, yet I could not endure that he should renew his grief by a recital of his misfortunes. I expressed these feelings in my answer.

He then told me that he would commence his narrative the next day when I should be at leisure. This promise drew from me the warmest thanks. I have resolved every night, when I am not imperatively occupied by my duties, to record, as nearly as possible in his own words, what he has related during the day. If I should be engaged, I will at least make notes. This manuscript will doubtless afford you the greatest pleasure; but to me, who know him, and who hear it from his own lips—with what interest and sympathy shall I read it in some future day!

Strange and harrowing must be his story, frightful the storm which embraced the gallant vessel on its course and wrecked it—thus!

My ancestors had been for many years counsellors and syndics, and my father had filled several public situations with honour and reputation. He was respected by all who knew him for his integrity and indefatigable attention to public business.

As the circumstances of his marriage illustrate his character, I cannot refrain from relating them. One of his most intimate friends was a merchant who, from a flourishing state, fell, through numerous mischances, into poverty. This man, whose name was Beaufort, was of a proud and unbending disposition and could not bear to live in poverty and oblivion in the same country where he had formerly been distinguished for his rank and magnificence. Having paid his debts, therefore, in the most honourable manner, he retreated with his daughter to the town of Lucerne, where he lived unknown and in wretchedness. My father loved Beaufort with the truest friendship and was deeply grieved by his retreat in these unfortunate circumstances. Beaufort had taken effectual measures to conceal himself, and it was ten months before my father discovered his abode.

Several months passed in this manner. Her father grew worse; her time was more entirely occupied in attending him; her means of subsistence decreased; and in the tenth month her father died in her arms, leaving her an orphan and a beggar. This last blow overcame her, and she knelt by Beaufort's coffin weeping bitterly, when my father entered the chamber. Two years after this event Caroline became his wife.

Everything was made to yield to her wishes and her convenience.

From Italy they visited Germany and France. I remained for several years their only child. My mother's tender caresses and my father's smile of benevolent pleasure while regarding me are my first recollections. For a long time I was their only care. Among these there was one which attracted my mother far above all the rest. Her hair was the brightest living gold, and despite the poverty of her clothing, seemed to set a crown of distinction on her head. The peasant woman, perceiving that my mother fixed eyes of wonder and admiration on this lovely girl, eagerly communicated her history. She was not her child, but the daughter of a Milanese nobleman. Her mother was a German and had died on giving her birth. The father of their charge was one of those Italians nursed in the memory of the antique glory of Italy—one among the schiavi ognor frementi, who exerted himself to obtain the liberty of his country. Whether he had died or still lingered in the dungeons of Austria was not known. His property was confiscated; his child became an orphan and a beggar. The apparition was soon explained. With his permission my mother prevailed on her rustic guardians to yield their charge to her. They were fond of the sweet orphan.

Everyone loved Elizabeth. All praises bestowed on her I received as made to a possession of my own. We called each other familiarly by the name of cousin.

We were brought up together; there was not quite a year difference in our ages. The world was to me a secret which I desired to divine.

Henry Clerval was the son of a merchant of Geneva. He was deeply read in books of chivalry and romance. He composed heroic songs and began to write many a tale of enchantment and knightly adventure.

No human being could have passed a happier childhood than myself.

The busy stage of life, the virtues of heroes, and the actions of men were his theme; and his hope and his dream was to become one among those whose names are recorded in story as the gallant and adventurous benefactors of our species. The saintly soul of Elizabeth shone like a shrine-dedicated lamp in our peaceful home. Her sympathy was ours; her smile, her soft voice, the sweet glance of her celestial eyes, were ever there to bless and animate us.

A new light seemed to dawn upon my mind, and bounding with joy, I communicated my discovery to my father. My father looked carelessly at the title page of my book and said, "Ah! Cornelius Agrippa! My dear Victor, do not waste your time upon this; it is sad trash."

Those of his successors in each branch of natural philosophy with whom I was acquainted appeared even to my boy's apprehensions as tyros engaged in the same pursuit.

The most learned philosopher knew little more.

My father was not scientific, and I was left to struggle with a child's blindness, added to a student's thirst for knowledge. Nor were these my only visions. When we visited it the next morning, we found the tree shattered in a singular manner. I never beheld anything so utterly destroyed.

Destiny was too potent, and her immutable laws had decreed my utter and terrible destruction.

Elizabeth had caught the scarlet fever; her illness was severe, and she was in the greatest danger. During her illness many arguments had been urged to persuade my mother to refrain from attending upon her. On the third day my mother sickened; her fever was accompanied by the most alarming symptoms, and the looks of her medical attendants prognosticated the worst event.

She died calmly, and her countenance expressed affection even in death.

I obtained from my father a respite of some weeks.

She indeed veiled her grief and strove to act the comforter to us all. Never was she so enchanting as at this time, when she recalled the sunshine of her smiles and spent them upon us. She forgot even her own regret in her endeavours to make us forget.

The day of my departure at length arrived. Clerval spent the last evening with us. He had endeavoured to persuade his father to permit him to accompany me and to become my fellow student, but in vain. His father was a narrow-minded trader and saw idleness and ruin in the aspirations and ambition of his son.

We sat late.

In the university whither I was going I must form my own friends and be my own protector. I ardently desired the acquisition of knowledge.

I had sufficient leisure for these and many other reflections during my journey to Ingolstadt, which was long and fatiguing. At length the high white steeple of the town met my eyes. I alighted and was conducted to my solitary apartment to spend the evening as I pleased.

Chance—or rather the evil influence, the Angel of Destruction, which asserted omnipotent sway over me from the moment I turned my reluctant steps from my father's door—led me first to M. Krempe, professor of natural philosophy. He was an uncouth man, but deeply imbued in the secrets of his science. The professor stared.

I replied in the affirmative.

M. Krempe was a little squat man with a gruff voice and a repulsive countenance; the teacher, therefore, did not prepossess me in favour of his pursuits. Besides, I had a contempt for the uses of modern natural philosophy. The ambition of the inquirer seemed to limit itself to the annihilation of those visions on which my interest in science was chiefly founded.

Such were my reflections during the first two or three days of my residence at Ingolstadt, which were chiefly spent in becoming acquainted with the localities and the principal residents in my new abode. But as the ensuing week commenced, I thought of the information which M. Krempe had given me concerning the lectures.

Partly from curiosity and partly from idleness, I went into the lecturing room, which M. Waldman entered shortly after. This professor was very unlike his colleague. His person was short but remarkably erect and his voice the sweetest I had ever heard.

By degrees, after the morning's dawn, sleep came. I awoke, and my yesternight's thoughts were as a dream. On the same day I paid M. Waldman a visit. His manners in private were even more mild and attractive than in public, for there was a certain dignity in his mien during his lecture which in his own house was replaced by the greatest affability and kindness. I gave him pretty nearly the same account of my former pursuits as I had given to his fellow professor. I requested his advice concerning the books I ought to procure.

In M. Waldman I found a true friend.

Professor Krempe often asked me, with a sly smile, how Cornelius

Agrippa went on, whilst M. Waldman expressed the most heartfelt exultation in my progress.

One of the phenomena which had peculiarly attracted my attention was the structure of the human frame, and, indeed, any animal endued with life. To examine the causes of life, we must first have recourse to death. My attention was fixed upon every object the most insupportable to the delicacy of the human feelings. I saw how the fine form of man was degraded and wasted; I beheld the corruption of death succeed to the blooming cheek of life; I saw how the worm inherited the wonders of the eye and brain.

Remember, I am not recording the vision of a madman.

I will not lead you on, unguarded and ardent as I then was, to your destruction and infallible misery.

When I found so astonishing a power placed within my hands, I hesitated a long time concerning the manner in which I should employ it. It was with these feelings that I began the creation of a human being.

Life and death appeared to me ideal bounds, which I should first break through, and pour a torrent of light into our dark world. A new species would bless me as its creator and source; many happy and excellent natures would owe their being to me. No father could claim the gratitude of his child so completely as I should deserve theirs.

Sometimes, on the very brink of certainty, I failed; yet still I clung to the hope which the next day or the next hour might realize. One secret which I alone possessed was the hope to which I had dedicated myself; and the moon gazed on my midnight labours, while, with unrelaxed and breathless eagerness, I pursued nature to her hiding-places. I collected bones from charnel-houses and disturbed, with profane fingers, the tremendous secrets of the human frame.

A human being in perfection ought always to preserve a calm and peaceful mind and never to allow passion or a transitory desire to disturb his tranquillity.

My father made no reproach in his letters and only took notice of my silence by inquiring into my occupations more particularly than before.

His limbs were in proportion, and I had selected his features as beautiful.

The different accidents of life are not so changeable as the feelings of human nature. I had worked hard for nearly two years, for the sole purpose of infusing life into an inanimate body. I thought I saw Elizabeth, in the bloom of health, walking in the streets of Ingolstadt. He held up the curtain of the bed; and his eyes, if eyes they may be called, were fixed on me. His jaws opened, and he muttered some inarticulate sounds, while a grin wrinkled his cheeks.

I passed the night wretchedly.

I traversed the streets without any clear conception of where I was or what I was doing.

Doth close behind him tread.

Here I paused, I knew not why; but I remained some minutes with my eyes fixed on a coach that was coming towards me from the other end of the street.

Nothing could equal my delight on seeing Clerval; his presence brought back to my thoughts my father, Elizabeth, and all those scenes of home so dear to my recollection. I grasped his hand, and in a moment forgot my horror and misfortune; I felt suddenly, and for the first time during many months, calm and serene joy. I welcomed my friend, therefore, in the most cordial manner, and we walked towards my college. Clerval continued talking for some time about our mutual friends and his own good fortune in being permitted to come to Ingolstadt.

"It gives me the greatest delight to see you; but tell me how you left my father, brothers, and Elizabeth."

My hand was already on the lock of the door before I recollected myself. I then paused, and a cold shivering came over me.

A meeting, which he anticipated with such joy, so strangely turned to bitterness. But I was not the witness of his grief, for I was lifeless and did not recover my senses for a long, long time.

During all that time Henry was my only nurse.

The form of the monster on whom I had bestowed existence was forever before my eyes, and I raved incessantly concerning him.

Clerval then put the following letter into my hands.

You are forbidden to write—to hold a pen; yet one word from you, dear Victor, is necessary to calm our apprehensions.

Get well—and return to us. You will find a happy, cheerful home and friends who love you dearly. Your father's health is vigorous, and he asks but to see you, but to be assured that you are well; and not a care will ever cloud his benevolent countenance. How pleased you would be to remark the improvement of our Ernest! He looks upon study as an odious fetter; his time is spent in the open air, climbing the hills or rowing on the lake.

Little alteration, except the growth of our dear children, has taken place since you left us. Since you left us, but one change has taken place in our little household. Probably you do not; I will relate her history, therefore in a few words. Madame Moritz, her mother, was a widow with four children, of whom Justine was the third. This girl had always been the favourite of her father, but through a strange perversity, her mother could not endure her, and after the death of M. Moritz, treated her very ill. My aunt observed this, and when Justine was twelve years of age, prevailed on her mother to allow her to live at our house. A servant in Geneva does not mean the same thing as a servant in France and England.

Although her disposition was gay and in many respects inconsiderate, yet she paid the greatest attention to every gesture of my aunt.

When my dearest aunt died every one was too much occupied in their own grief to notice poor Justine, who had attended her during her illness with the most anxious affection. Poor Justine was very ill; but other trials were reserved for her.

One by one, her brothers and sister died; and her mother, with the exception of her neglected daughter, was left childless. The conscience of the woman was troubled; she began to think that the deaths of her favourites was a judgement from heaven to chastise her partiality. She was a Roman Catholic; and I believe her confessor confirmed the idea which she had conceived. Accordingly, a few months after your departure for Ingolstadt, Justine was called home by her repentant mother. Nor was her residence at her mother's house of a nature to restore her gaiety. The poor woman was very vacillating in her repentance. Perpetual fretting at length threw Madame Moritz into a decline, which at first increased her irritability, but she is now at peace for ever. Justine has just returned to us; and I assure you I love her tenderly.

I wish you could see him; he is very tall of his age, with sweet laughing blue eyes, dark eyelashes, and curling hair. He has already had one or two little WIVES, but Louisa Biron is his favourite, a pretty little girl of five years of age.

Now, dear Victor, I dare say you wish to be indulged in a little gossip concerning the good people of Geneva. The pretty Miss Mansfield has already received the congratulatory visits on her approaching marriage with a young Englishman, John Melbourne, Esq. Her ugly sister, Manon, married M. Duvillard, the rich banker, last autumn. Your favourite schoolfellow, Louis Manoir, has suffered several misfortunes since the departure of Clerval from Geneva. But he has already recovered his spirits, and is reported to be on the point of marrying a lively pretty Frenchwoman, Madame Tavernier.

Write, dearest Victor,—one line—one word will be a blessing to us. Ten thousand thanks to Henry for his kindness, his affection, and his many letters; we are sincerely grateful. my cousin; take care of your self; and, I entreat you, write!

"Geneva, March 18, 17—."

In another fortnight I was able to leave my chamber.

One of my first duties on my recovery was to introduce Clerval to the several professors of the university. When I was otherwise quite restored to health, the sight of a chemical instrument would renew all the agony of my nervous symptoms. M. Waldman inflicted torture when he praised, with kindness and warmth, the astonishing progress I had made in the sciences. I writhed under his words, yet dared not exhibit the pain I felt.

M. Krempe was not equally docile; and in my condition at that time, of almost insupportable sensitiveness, his harsh blunt encomiums gave me even more pain than the benevolent approbation of M. Waldman.

Resolved to pursue no inglorious career, he turned his eyes toward the East, as affording scope for his spirit of enterprise. The Persian, Arabic, and Sanskrit languages engaged his attention, and I was easily induced to enter on the same studies.How different from the manly and heroical poetry of Greece and Rome!

You have probably waited impatiently for a letter to fix the date of your return to us; and I was at first tempted to write only a few lines, merely mentioning the day on which I should expect you. But that would be a cruel kindness, and I dare not do it.

William is dead! Victor, he is murdered!

Last Thursday (May 7th), I, my niece, and your two brothers, went to walk in Plainpalais. We accordingly rested on a seat until they should return.

He was not there. About five in the morning I discovered my lovely boy, whom the night before I had seen blooming and active in health, stretched on the grass livid and motionless; the print of the murder's finger was on his neck.

She was very earnest to see the corpse. I have murdered my darling child! '

Come, dearest Victor; you alone can console Elizabeth. She weeps continually, and accuses herself unjustly as the cause of his death; her words pierce my heart. Your dear mother! I now say, Thank God she did not live to witness the cruel, miserable death of her youngest darling!

During our walk, Clerval endeavoured to say a few words of consolation; he could only express his heartfelt sympathy.

My journey was very melancholy. How altered every thing might be during that time!

I discovered more distinctly the black sides of Jura, and the bright summit of Mont Blanc. I wept like a child.

My country, my beloved country!

The sky was serene; and, as I was unable to rest, I resolved to visit the spot where my poor William had been murdered. As I could not pass through the town, I was obliged to cross the lake in a boat to arrive at Plainpalais.

The storm, as is often the case in Switzerland, appeared at once in various parts of the heavens.

Nothing in human shape could have destroyed the fair child. He was the murderer! I could not doubt it. The mere presence of the idea was an irresistible proof of the fact.

I remained motionless.

Day dawned; and I directed my steps towards the town. The gates were open, and I hastened to my father's house. My first thought was to discover what I knew of the murderer, and cause instant pursuit to be made. But I paused when I reflected on the story that I had to tell. A being whom I myself had formed, and endued with life, had met me at midnight among the precipices of an inaccessible mountain.

It was about five in the morning when I entered my father's house.

Beloved and venerable parent! I gazed on the picture of my mother, which stood over the mantel-piece. It was an historical subject, painted at my father's desire, and represented Caroline Beaufort in an agony of despair, kneeling by the coffin of her dead father. While I was thus engaged, Ernest entered: he had heard me arrive, and hastened to welcome me: "Welcome, my dearest Victor," said he. "Ah! I wish you had come three months ago, and then you would have found us all joyous and delighted. You come to us now to share a misery which nothing can alleviate; yet your presence will, I hope, revive our father, who seems sinking under his misfortune; and your persuasions will induce poor Elizabeth to cease her vain and tormenting self-accusations.—Poor William! he was our darling and our pride!"

Tears, unrestrained, fell from my brother's eyes; a sense of mortal agony crept over my frame. I tried to calm Ernest; I enquired more minutely concerning my father, and here I named my cousin.

On being charged with the fact, the poor girl confirmed the suspicion in a great measure by her extreme confusion of manner.

At that instant my father entered.

"My dear father, you are mistaken; Justine is innocent."

This speech calmed me.

We were soon joined by Elizabeth. Time had altered her since I last beheld her; it had endowed her with loveliness surpassing the beauty of her childish years.

We passed a few sad hours until eleven o'clock, when the trial was to commence. My father and the rest of the family being obliged to attend as witnesses, I accompanied them to the court. Justine also was a girl of merit and possessed qualities which promised to render her life happy; now all was to be obliterated in an ignominious grave, and I the cause!

The appearance of Justine was calm. When she entered the court she threw her eyes round it and quickly discovered where we were seated.

The trial began, and after the advocate against her had stated the charge, several witnesses were called. Several strange facts combined against her, which might have staggered anyone who had not such proof of her innocence as I had. The woman asked her what she did there, but she looked very strangely and only returned a confused and unintelligible answer. When shown the body, she fell into violent hysterics and kept her bed for several days.

Justine was called on for her defence. As the trial had proceeded, her countenance had altered.

On her return, at about nine o'clock, she met a man who asked her if she had seen anything of the child who was lost. If she had gone near the spot where his body lay, it was without her knowledge.That she had been bewildered when questioned by the market-woman was not surprising, since she had passed a sleepless night and the fate of poor William was yet uncertain. Concerning the picture she could give no account.

My own agitation and anguish was extreme during the whole trial. I believed in her innocence; I knew it.

I passed a night of unmingled wretchedness. In the morning I went to the court; my lips and throat were parched. The ballots had been thrown; they were all black, and Justine was condemned.

I cannot pretend to describe what I then felt.The person to whom I addressed myself added that Justine had already confessed her guilt.

I hastened to return home, and Elizabeth eagerly demanded the result.

This was a dire blow to poor Elizabeth, who had relied with firmness upon Justine's innocence."Alas!" said she.

"Yes," said Elizabeth, "I will go, although she is guilty; and you, Victor, shall accompany me; I cannot go alone." The idea of this visit was torture to me, yet I could not refuse. We entered the gloomy prison chamber and beheld Justine sitting on some straw at the farther end; her hands were manacled, and her head rested on her knees. My cousin wept also.

"Oh, Justine!" said she.

Justine shook her head mournfully.

The poor victim, who on the morrow was to pass the awful boundary between life and death, felt not, as I did, such deep and bitter agony.

I could not answer.

Justine assumed an air of cheerfulness, while she with difficulty repressed her bitter tears.

And on the morrow Justine died.

From the tortures of my own heart, I turned to contemplate the deep and voiceless grief of my Elizabeth. Ye weep, unhappy ones, but these are not your last tears! Again shall you raise the funeral wail, and the sound of your lamentations shall again and again be heard!

Justine died, she rested, and I was alive. Sleep fled from my eyes; I wandered like an evil spirit, for I had committed deeds of mischief beyond description horrible, and more, much more (I persuaded myself) was yet behind.

I shunned the face of man; all sound of joy or complacency was torture to me; solitude was my only consolation—deep, dark, deathlike solitude.

Now I could only answer my father with a look of despair and endeavour to hide myself from his view.

About this time we retired to our house at Belrive. This change was particularly agreeable to me. I was now free. Often, after the rest of the family had retired for the night, I took the boat and passed many hours upon the water.

Remorse extinguished every hope. There was always scope for fear so long as anything I loved remained behind. When I thought of him I gnashed my teeth, my eyes became inflamed, and I ardently wished to extinguish that life which I had so thoughtlessly bestowed. When I reflected on his crimes and malice, my hatred and revenge burst all bounds of moderation. Our house was the house of mourning. My father's health was deeply shaken by the horror of the recent events. The first of those sorrows which are sent to wean us from the earth had visited her, and its dimming influence quenched her dearest smiles.

I was encompassed by a cloud which no beneficial influence could penetrate.

My wanderings were directed towards the valley of Chamounix.

I performed the first part of my journey on horseback.

At length I arrived at the village of Chamounix.

I spent the following day roaming through the valley.

My mule was brought to the door, and I resolved to ascend to the summit of Montanvert.

It is a scene terrifically desolate.

We rest; a dream has power to poison sleep. We rise; one wand'ring thought pollutes the day. The path of its departure still is free.

It was nearly noon when I arrived at the top of the ascent. For some time I sat upon the rock that overlooks the sea of ice. The opposite mountain is a bare perpendicular rock.

As I said this I suddenly beheld the figure of a man, at some distance, advancing towards me with superhuman speed. I trembled with rage and horror, resolving to wait his approach and then close with him in mortal combat.

For the first time, also, I felt what the duties of a creator towards his creature were, and that I ought to render him happy before I complained of his wickedness. These motives urged me to comply with his demand.

By degrees, I remember, a stronger light pressed upon my nerves, so that I was obliged to shut my eyes. This was the forest near Ingolstadt; and here I lay by the side of a brook resting from my fatigue, until I felt tormented by hunger and thirst.

[The moon] I gazed with a kind of wonder. No distinct ideas occupied my mind; all was confused.

Sometimes I tried to imitate the pleasant songs of the birds but was unable.

When night came on and brought sleep with it, I was in the greatest fear lest my fire should be extinguished.

It was morning when I awoke, and my first care was to visit the fire. I tried, therefore, to dress my food in the same manner, placing it on the live embers.

Finding the door open, I entered. An old man sat in it, near a fire, over which he was preparing his breakfast.

Having thus arranged my dwelling and carpeted it with clean straw, I retired, for I saw the figure of a man at a distance, and I remembered too well my treatment the night before to trust myself in his power.

Presently I saw the young man again, with some tools in his hand, cross the field behind the cottage; and the girl was also busied, sometimes in the house and sometimes in the yard.

In one corner, near a small fire, sat an old man, leaning his head on his hands in a disconsolate attitude. He played a sweet mournful air which I perceived drew tears from the eyes of his amiable companion, of which the old man took no notice, until she sobbed audibly; he then pronounced a few sounds, and the fair creature, leaving her work, knelt at his feet.

Soon after this the young man returned, bearing on his shoulders a load of wood. She afterwards continued her work, whilst the young man went into the garden and appeared busily employed in digging and pulling up roots.

The old man had, in the meantime, been pensive, but on the appearance of his companions he assumed a more cheerful air, and they sat down to eat. The meal was quickly dispatched. The young woman was again occupied in arranging the cottage, the old man walked before the cottage in the sun for a few minutes, leaning on the arm of the youth. The old man returned to the cottage, and the youth, with tools different from those he had used in the morning, directed his steps across the fields.

I lay on my straw, but I could not sleep. I thought of the occurrences of the day. What chiefly struck me was the gentle manners of these people, and I longed to join them, but dared not.

The cottagers arose the next morning before the sun. The young woman arranged the cottage and prepared the food, and the youth departed after the first meal.

The young man was constantly employed out of doors, and the girl in various laborious occupations within. The old man, whom I soon perceived to be blind, employed his leisure hours on his instrument or in contemplation.

They were not entirely happy. The young man and his companion often went apart and appeared to weep. I was at first unable to solve these questions, but perpetual attention and time explained to me many appearances which were at first enigmatic.

I remember, the first time that I did this, the young woman, when she opened the door in the morning, appeared greatly astonished on seeing a great pile of wood on the outside.

By degrees I made a discovery of still greater moment. The youth and his companion had each of them several names, but the old man had only one, which was 'father.' The girl was called 'sister' or 'Agatha,' and the youth 'Felix,' 'brother,' or 'son.'

I spent the winter in this manner. The old man, I could perceive, often endeavoured to encourage his children, as sometimes I found that he called them, to cast off their melancholy. It was not thus with Felix.

In the day, I believe, he worked sometimes for a neighbouring farmer, because he often went forth and did not return until dinner, yet brought no wood with him. At other times he worked in the garden, but as there was little to do in the frosty season, he read to the old man and Agatha.

My mode of life in my hovel was uniform.

When I slept or was absent, the forms of the venerable blind father, the gentle Agatha, and the excellent Felix flitted before me.

I now hasten to the more moving part of my story.

Felix replied in a cheerful accent, and the old man was recommencing his music when someone tapped at the door.

It was a lady on horseback, accompanied by a country-man as a guide.

He assisted her to dismount, and dismissing her guide, conducted her into the cottage. Some conversation took place between him and his father, and the young stranger knelt at the old man's feet and would have kissed his hand, but he raised her and embraced her affectionately.

They made many signs which I did not comprehend, but I saw that her presence diffused gladness through the cottage, dispelling their sorrow as the sun dissipates the morning mists.Felix seemed peculiarly happy and with smiles of delight welcomed his Arabian.

As night came on, Agatha and the Arabian retired early. When they separated Felix kissed the hand of the stranger and said, 'Good night sweet Safie.' He sat up much longer, conversing with his father, and by the frequent repetition of her name I conjectured that their lovely guest was the subject of their conversation.

She sang, and her voice flowed in a rich cadence, swelling or dying away like a nightingale of the woods.

When she had finished, she gave the guitar to Agatha, who at first declined it.

The book from which Felix instructed Safie was Volney's Ruins of Empires.

For a long time I could not conceive how one man could go forth to murder his fellow, or even why there were laws and governments; but when I heard details of vice and bloodshed, my wonder ceased and I turned away with disgust and loathing.

Every conversation of the cottagers now opened new wonders to me. While I listened to the instructions which Felix bestowed upon the Arabian, the strange system of human society was explained to me.

The words induced me to turn towards myself. I was, besides, endued with a figure hideously deformed and loathsome; I was not even of the same nature as man. When I looked around I saw and heard of none like me.

Of what a strange nature is knowledge! The mild exhortations of the old man and the lively conversation of the loved Felix were not for me. Miserable, unhappy wretch!

Other lessons were impressed upon me even more deeply.

No father had watched my infant days, no mother had blessed me with smiles and caresses; or if they had, all my past life was now a blot, a blind vacancy in which I distinguished nothing. From my earliest remembrance I had been as I then was in height and proportion. The question again recurred, to be answered only with groans.

Some time elapsed before I learned the history of my friends.

The name of the old man was De Lacey. He was descended from a good family in France, where he had lived for many years in affluence, respected by his superiors and beloved by his equals. His son was bred in the service of his country, and Agatha had ranked with ladies of the highest distinction.

The father of Safie had been the cause of their ruin.

Felix visited the grate at night and made known to the prisoner his intentions in his favour. The Turk, amazed and delighted, endeavoured to kindle the zeal of his deliverer by promises of reward and wealth.

She thanked him in the most ardent terms for his intended services towards her parent, and at the same time she gently deplored her own fate.

Safie related that her mother was a Christian Arab, seized and made a slave by the Turks; recommended by her beauty, she had won the heart of the father of Safie, who married her.

The day for the execution of the Turk was fixed, but on the night previous to it he quitted his prison and before morning was distant many leagues from Paris. Felix had procured passports in the name of his father, sister, and himself.

They conversed with one another through the means of an interpreter, and sometimes with the interpretation of looks; and Safie sang to him the divine airs of her native country.

His plans were facilitated by the news which arrived from Paris.

The government of France were greatly enraged at the escape of their victim and spared no pains to detect and punish his deliverer. The plot of Felix was quickly discovered, and De Lacey and Agatha were thrown into prison. The news reached Felix and roused him from his dream of pleasure. His blind and aged father and his gentle sister lay in a noisome dungeon while he enjoyed the free air and the society of her whom he loved. This idea was torture to him.

He did not succeed.

They found a miserable asylum in the cottage in Germany, where I discovered them.

Such were the events that preyed on the heart of Felix and rendered him, when I first saw him, the most miserable of his family. The arrival of the Arabian now infused new life into his soul.

When the news reached Leghorn that Felix was deprived of his wealth and rank, the merchant commanded his daughter to think no more of her lover, but to prepare to return to her native country. The generous nature of Safie was outraged by this command; she attempted to expostulate with her father, but he left her angrily, reiterating his tyrannical mandate.

He intended to leave his daughter under the care of a confidential servant, to follow at her leisure with the greater part of his property, which had not yet arrived at Leghorn.

A residence in Turkey was abhorrent to her; her religion and her feelings were alike averse to it. By some papers of her father which fell into her hands she heard of the exile of her lover and learnt the name of the spot where he then resided. She hesitated some time, but at length she formed her determination.

Such was the history of my beloved cottagers. I learned, from the views of social life which it developed, to admire their virtues and to deprecate the vices of mankind.

One night during my accustomed visit to the neighbouring wood where I collected my own food and brought home firing for my protectors, I found on the ground a leathern portmanteau containing several articles of dress and some books.

I can hardly describe to you the effect of these books.

As I read, however, I applied much personally to my own feelings and condition. I found myself similar yet at the same time strangely unlike to the beings concerning whom I read and to whose conversation I was a listener. My person was hideous and my stature gigantic. These questions continually recurred, but I was unable to solve them.

The volume of Plutarch's Lives which I possessed contained the histories of the first founders of the ancient republics. This book had a far different effect upon me from the Sorrows of Werter. Many things I read surpassed my understanding and experience. The cottage of my protectors had been the only school in which I had studied human nature, but this book developed new and mightier scenes of action. Induced by these feelings, I was of course led to admire peaceable lawgivers, Numa, Solon, and Lycurgus, in preference to Romulus and Theseus. The patriarchal lives of my protectors caused these impressions to take a firm hold on my mind; perhaps, if my first introduction to humanity had been made by a young soldier, burning for glory and slaughter, I should have been imbued with different sensations.

Like Adam, I was apparently united by no link to any other being in existence; but his state was far different from mine in every other respect. Many times I considered Satan as the fitter emblem of my condition, for often, like him, when I viewed the bliss of my protectors, the bitter gall of envy rose within me.

Soon after my arrival in the hovel I discovered some papers in the pocket of the dress which I had taken from your laboratory. You doubtless recollect these papers. Here they are. I sickened as I read. 'Hateful day when I received life! ' I exclaimed in agony. God, in pity, made man beautiful and alluring, after his own image; but my form is a filthy type of yours, more horrid even from the very resemblance. Satan had his companions, fellow devils, to admire and encourage him, but I am solitary and abhorred. '

Several changes, in the meantime, took place in the cottage. Increase of knowledge only discovered to me more clearly what a wretched outcast I was.

Autumn passed thus. Their happiness was not decreased by the absence of summer.

The winter advanced, and an entire revolution of the seasons had taken place since I awoke into life. My attention at this time was solely directed towards my plan of introducing myself into the cottage of my protectors. My voice, although harsh, had nothing terrible in it; I thought, therefore, that if in the absence of his children I could gain the good will and mediation of the old De Lacey, I might by his means be tolerated by my younger protectors.

The servants were gone to a neighbouring fair.

'Enter,' said De Lacey, 'and I will try in what manner I can to relieve your wants; but, unfortunately, my children are from home, and as I am blind, I am afraid I shall find it difficult to procure food for you. '

I sat down, and a silence ensued. I knew that every minute was precious to me, yet I remained irresolute in what manner to commence the interview, when the old man addressed me. '

'No, they are French. But let us change the subject. I am full of fears, for if I fail there, I am an outcast in the world forever. '

'Do not despair. '

The old man paused and then continued, 'If you will unreservedly confide to me the particulars of your tale, I perhaps may be of use in undeceiving them. '

I thank you and accept your generous offer. '

From your lips first have I heard the voice of kindness directed towards me; I shall be forever grateful; and your present humanity assures me of success with those friends whom I am on the point of meeting. '

At that moment I heard the steps of my younger protectors. I had not a moment to lose, but seizing the hand of the old man, I cried, 'Now is the time!Save and protect me! You and your family are the friends whom I seek. Do not you desert me in the hour of trial! '

Cursed, cursed creator!

What a miserable night I passed!

I had certainly acted imprudently.

The horrible scene of the preceding day was forever acting before my eyes; the females were flying and the enraged Felix tearing me from his father's feet.

All there was at peace. I trembled violently, apprehending some dreadful misfortune.

Soon after, however, Felix approached with another man; I was surprised, as I knew that he had not quitted the cottage that morning, and waited anxiously to discover from his discourse the meaning of these unusual appearances.

'It is utterly useless,' replied Felix; 'we can never again inhabit your cottage. The life of my father is in the greatest danger, owing to the dreadful circumstance that I have related. I entreat you not to reason with me any more. '

I never saw any of the family of De Lacey more.

At length the thought of you crossed my mind.

Unfeeling, heartless creator! You had endowed me with perceptions and passions and then cast me abroad an object for the scorn and horror of mankind.

My travels were long and the sufferings I endured intense. It was late in autumn when I quitted the district where I had so long resided. I travelled only at night, fearful of encountering the visage of a human being. How often did I imprecate curses on the cause of my being! The nearer I approached to your habitation, the more deeply did I feel the spirit of revenge enkindled in my heart.

I generally rested during the day and travelled only when I was secured by night from the view of man.

I followed speedily, I hardly knew why; but when the man saw me draw near, he aimed a gun, which he carried, at my body and fired.

This was then the reward of my benevolence! I had saved a human being from destruction, and as a recompense I now writhed under the miserable pain of a wound which shattered the flesh and bone. Inflamed by pain, I vowed eternal hatred and vengeance to all mankind. But the agony of my wound overcame me; my pulses paused, and I fainted.

For some weeks I led a miserable life in the woods, endeavouring to cure the wound which I had received.

"I do not intend to hurt you; listen to me."

"Let me go," he cried; "monster! You wish to eat me and tear me to pieces. You are an ogre. Let me go, or I will tell my papa."

"Boy, you will never see your father again; you must come with me. "

"Let me go. My papa is a syndic—he is M. Frankenstein—he will punish you. You dare not keep me."

You belong then to my enemy—to him towards whom I have sworn eternal revenge; you shall be my first victim. '

As I fixed my eyes on the child, I saw something glittering on his breast. I took it; it was a portrait of a most lovely woman.

A woman was sleeping on some straw; she was young, not indeed so beautiful as her whose portrait I held, but of an agreeable aspect and blooming in the loveliness of youth and health. And then I bent over her and whispered, "Awake, fairest, thy lover is near—he who would give his life but to obtain one look of affection from thine eyes; my beloved, awake!"

The sleeper stirred; a thrill of terror ran through me. The crime had its source in her; be hers the punishment! Thanks to the lessons of Felix and the sanguinary laws of man, I had learned now to work mischief. I bent over her and placed the portrait securely in one of the folds of her dress.

The being finished speaking and fixed his looks upon me in the expectation of a reply. But I was bewildered, perplexed, and unable to arrange my ideas sufficiently to understand the full extent of his proposition.

I was moved.

His words had a strange effect upon me.

I thought of the promise of virtues which he had displayed on the opening of his existence and the subsequent blight of all kindly feeling by the loathing and scorn which his protectors had manifested towards him. After a long pause of reflection I concluded that the justice due both to him and my fellow creatures demanded of me that I should comply with his request.

"I consent to your demand, on your solemn oath to quit Europe forever, and every other place in the neighbourhood of man, as soon as I shall deliver into your hands a female who will accompany you in your exile."

Saying this, he suddenly quitted me, fearful, perhaps, of any change in my sentiments.

Night was far advanced when I came to the halfway resting-place and seated myself beside the fountain.

Morning dawned before I arrived at the village of Chamounix; I took no rest, but returned immediately to Geneva.

Day after day, week after week, passed away on my return to Geneva; and I could not collect the courage to recommence my work. At these moments I took refuge in the most perfect solitude.

I trembled violently at his exordium, and my father continued—"I confess, my son, that I have always looked forward to your marriage with our dear Elizabeth as the tie of our domestic comfort and the stay of my declining years. You, perhaps, regard her as your sister, without any wish that she might become your wife. "

"My dear father, reassure yourself. I love my cousin tenderly and sincerely. I never saw any woman who excited, as Elizabeth does, my warmest admiration and affection. My future hopes and prospects are entirely bound up in the expectation of our union."

I listened to my father in silence and remained for some time incapable of offering any reply. To me the idea of an immediate union with my Elizabeth was one of horror and dismay. I was bound by a solemn promise which I had not yet fulfilled and dared not break, or if I did, what manifold miseries might not impend over me and my devoted family! I must perform my engagement and let the monster depart with his mate before I allowed myself to enjoy the delight of a union from which I expected peace.

I must absent myself from all I loved while thus employed. My promise fulfilled, the monster would depart forever.

These feelings dictated my answer to my father.

My father's age rendered him extremely averse to delay.

It had been her care which provided me a companion in Clerval—and yet a man is blind to a thousand minute circumstances which call forth a woman's sedulous attention.

Filled with dreary imaginations, I passed through many beautiful and majestic scenes, but my eyes were fixed and unobserving.

After some days spent in listless indolence, during which I traversed many leagues, I arrived at Strasbourg, where I waited two days for Clerval. Alas, how great was the contrast between us!

We had agreed to descend the Rhine in a boat from Strasbourg to Rotterdam, whence we might take shipping for London. We stayed a day at Mannheim, and on the fifth from our departure from Strasbourg, arrived at Mainz. The course of the Rhine below Mainz becomes much more picturesque. We saw many ruined castles standing on the edges of precipices, surrounded by black woods, high and inaccessible.

His soul overflowed with ardent affections, and his friendship was of that devoted and wondrous nature that the world-minded teach us to look for only in the imagination. But even human sympathies were not sufficient to satisfy his eager mind.

Unborrow'd from the eye.

I will proceed with my tale.

We saw Tilbury Fort and remembered the Spanish Armada, Gravesend, Woolwich, and Greenwich—places which I had heard of even in my country.

At length we saw the numerous steeples of London, St. Paul's towering above all, and the Tower famed in English history.

The difference of manners which he observed was to him an inexhaustible source of instruction and amusement. In Britain only could he further the execution of his plan. He was forever busy, and the only check to his enjoyments was my sorrowful and dejected mind.

We had arrived in England at the beginning of October, and it was now February.

From thence we proceeded to Oxford. It was here that Charles I. had collected his forces. This city had remained faithful to him, after the whole nation had forsaken his cause to join the standard of Parliament and liberty.

I was formed for peaceful happiness.

We left Oxford with regret and proceeded to Matlock, which was our next place of rest.

From Derby, still journeying northwards, we passed two months in Cumberland and Westmorland. I could now almost fancy myself among the Swiss mountains. "I could pass my life here," said he to me; "and among these mountains I should scarcely regret Switzerland and the Rhine."

For my own part I was not sorry.

Clerval did not like it so well as Oxford, for the antiquity of the latter city was more pleasing to him. But the beauty and regularity of the new town of Edinburgh, its romantic castle and its environs, the most delightful in the world, Arthur's Seat, St. Bernard's Well, and the Pentland Hills compensated him for the change and filled him with cheerfulness and admiration. But I was impatient to arrive at the termination of my journey.

On the whole island there were but three miserable huts, and one of these was vacant when I arrived.

It was a monotonous yet ever-changing scene.

Sometimes I could not prevail on myself to enter my laboratory for several days, and at other times I toiled day and night in order to complete my work. It was, indeed, a filthy process in which I was engaged.

Every moment I feared to meet my persecutor.Sometimes I sat with my eyes fixed on the ground, fearing to raise them lest they should encounter the object which I so much dreaded to behold. I feared to wander from the sight of my fellow creatures lest when alone he should come to claim his companion.

In the mean time I worked on, and my labour was already considerably advanced.

As I sat, a train of reflection occurred to me which led me to consider the effects of what I was now doing.

A ghastly grin wrinkled his lips as he gazed on me, where I sat fulfilling the task which he had allotted to me.

As I looked on him, his countenance expressed the utmost extent of malice and treachery.

The monster saw my determination in my face and gnashed his teeth in the impotence of anger.

It is well. I go; but remember, I shall be with you on your wedding-night."

In a few moments I saw him in his boat, which shot across the waters with an arrowy swiftness and was soon lost amidst the waves.

All was again silent, but his words rang in my ears. I shuddered to think who might be the next victim sacrificed to his insatiate revenge. And then I thought again of his words—"I WILL BE WITH YOU ON YOUR WEDDING-NIGHT." That, then, was the period fixed for the fulfilment of my destiny. In that hour I should die and at once satisfy and extinguish his malice. The prospect did not move me to fear; yet when I thought of my beloved Elizabeth, of her tears and endless sorrow, when she should find her lover so barbarously snatched from her, tears, the first I had shed for many months, streamed from my eyes, and I resolved not to fall before my enemy without a bitter struggle.

I had been awake the whole of the preceding night, my nerves were agitated, and my eyes inflamed by watching and misery.

The remains of the half-finished creature, whom I had destroyed, lay scattered on the floor, and I almost felt as if I had mangled the living flesh of a human being.

I had already been out many hours and felt the torment of a burning thirst, a prelude to my other sufferings. "Fiend," I exclaimed, "your task is already fulfilled!" I thought of Elizabeth, of my father, and of Clerval—all left behind, on whom the monster might satisfy his sanguinary and merciless passions.

I saw vessels near the shore and found myself suddenly transported back to the neighbourhood of civilized man. Fortunately I had money with me.

"You will know that soon enough," replied a man with a hoarse voice.

I then moved forward, and a murmuring sound arose from the crowd as they followed and surrounded me, when an ill-looking man approaching tapped me on the shoulder and said, "Come, sir, you must follow me to Mr. Kirwin's to give an account of yourself."

Ay, sir, free enough for honest folks. Mr. Kirwin is a magistrate, and you are to give an account of the death of a gentleman who was found murdered here last night."

I was soon introduced into the presence of the magistrate, an old benevolent man with calm and mild manners.

He walked on first, carrying a part of the fishing tackle, and his companions followed him at some distance.

As he was proceeding along the sands, he struck his foot against something and fell at his length on the ground. It appeared to be a handsome young man, about five and twenty years of age. He had apparently been strangled, for there was no sign of any violence except the black mark of fingers on his neck.

The magistrate observed me with a keen eye and of course drew an unfavourable augury from my manner.

Another woman confirmed the account of the fishermen having brought the body into her house; it was not cold.

Two I have already destroyed; other victims await their destiny; but you, Clerval, my friend, my benefactor—"

The human frame could no longer support the agonies that I endured, and I was carried out of the room in strong convulsions. A fever succeeded to this.

This sound disturbed an old woman who was sleeping in a chair beside me.

One day, while I was gradually recovering, I was seated in a chair, my eyes half open and my cheeks livid like those in death. Such were my thoughts when the door of my apartment was opened and Mr. Kirwin entered.

"Your family is perfectly well," said Mr. Kirwin with gentleness; "and someone, a friend, is come to visit you."

I put my hand before my eyes, and cried out in agony, "Oh! Take him away! I cannot see him; for God's sake, do not let him enter!"

Mr. Kirwin regarded me with a troubled countenance.

"My father!" cried I, while every feature and every muscle was relaxed from anguish to pleasure.

And poor Clerval—"

"Alas! Yes, my father," replied I; "some destiny of the most horrible kind hangs over me, and I must live to fulfil it, or surely I should have died on the coffin of Henry."

The image of Clerval was forever before me, ghastly and murdered.

The season of the assizes approached.

My father tried to awaken in me the feelings of affection.

My father still desired to delay our departure, fearful that I could not sustain the fatigues of a journey, for I was a shattered wreck—the shadow of a human being. My strength was gone. I was a mere skeleton, and fever night and day preyed upon my wasted frame. Still, as I urged our leaving Ireland with such inquietude and impatience, my father thought it best to yield.

The voyage came to an end. We landed, and proceeded to Paris. I abhorred the face of man.Oh, not abhorred!

"Alas! My father," said I, "how little do you know me. Human beings, their feelings and passions, would indeed be degraded if such a wretch as I felt pride. Justine, poor unhappy Justine, was as innocent as I, and she suffered the same charge; she died for it; and I am the cause of this—I murdered her. William, Justine, and Henry—they all died by my hands."

As time passed away I became more calm; misery had her dwelling in my heart, but I no longer talked in the same incoherent manner of my own crimes; sufficient for me was the consciousness of them.

You well know, Victor, that our union had been the favourite plan of your parents ever since our infancy. Tell me, dearest Victor.

This letter revived in my memory what I had before forgotten, the threat of the fiend—"I WILL BE WITH YOU ON YOUR WEDDING-NIGHT!" On that night he had determined to consummate his crimes by my death. Well, be it so; a deadly struggle would then assuredly take place, in which if he were victorious I should be at peace and his power over me be at an end. If he were vanquished, I should be a free man.

Sweet and beloved Elizabeth! Yet I would die to make her happy. If the monster executed his threat, death was inevitable; yet, again, I considered whether my marriage would hasten my fate.

He had vowed TO BE WITH ME ON MY WEDDING-NIGHT, yet he did not consider that threat as binding him to peace in the meantime, for as if to show me that he was not yet satiated with blood, he had murdered Clerval immediately after the enunciation of his threats.

In this state of mind I wrote to Elizabeth. My letter was calm and affectionate.

In about a week after the arrival of Elizabeth's letter we returned to Geneva. The sweet girl welcomed me with warm affection, yet tears were in her eyes as she beheld my emaciated frame and feverish cheeks. I saw a change in her also. The tranquillity which I now enjoyed did not endure.

Elizabeth alone had the power to draw me from these fits; her gentle voice would soothe me when transported by passion and inspire me with human feelings when sunk in torpor. The agonies of remorse poison the luxury there is otherwise sometimes found in indulging the excess of grief.Soon after my arrival my father spoke of my immediate marriage with Elizabeth. I remained silent.

"None on earth. I love Elizabeth and look forward to our union with delight. Let the day therefore be fixed; and on it I will consecrate myself, in life or death, to the happiness of my cousin."

Such were the lessons of my father.

Through my father's exertions a part of the inheritance of Elizabeth had been restored to her by the Austrian government. A small possession on the shores of Como belonged to her.

In the meantime I took every precaution to defend my person in case the fiend should openly attack me.

My father was in the meantime overjoyed and in the bustle of preparation only recognized in the melancholy of his niece the diffidence of a bride.

The day was fair, the wind favourable; all smiled on our nuptial embarkation.

Those were the last moments of my life during which I enjoyed the feeling of happiness.

I took the hand of Elizabeth.

Thus Elizabeth endeavoured to divert her thoughts and mine from all reflection upon melancholy subjects. But her temper was fluctuating; joy for a few instants shone in her eyes, but it continually gave place to distraction and reverie.

Suddenly a heavy storm of rain descended.

It came from the room into which Elizabeth had retired. Why did I not then expire! She was there, lifeless and inanimate, thrown across the bed, her head hanging down and her pale and distorted features half covered by her hair. Life is obstinate and clings closest where it is most hated. For a moment only did I lose recollection; I fell senseless on the ground.

She had been moved from the posture in which I had first beheld her, and now, as she lay, her head upon her arm and a handkerchief thrown across her face and neck, I might have supposed her asleep. The murderous mark of the fiend's grasp was on her neck, and the breath had ceased to issue from her lips. While I still hung over her in the agony of despair, I happened to look up. A grin was on the face of the monster; he seemed to jeer, as with his fiendish finger he pointed towards the corpse of my wife.

The report of the pistol brought a crowd into the room.

I was bewildered, in a cloud of wonder and horror. The death of William, the execution of Justine, the murder of Clerval, and lastly of my wife; even at that moment I knew not that my only remaining friends were safe from the malignity of the fiend; my father even now might be writhing under his grasp, and Ernest might be dead at his feet.

If I looked up, I saw scenes which were familiar to me in my happier time and which I had contemplated but the day before in the company of her who was now but a shadow and a recollection. Tears streamed from my eyes. Nothing is so painful to the human mind as a great and sudden change. Know that, one by one, my friends were snatched away; I was left desolate. I arrived at Geneva. I see him now, excellent and venerable old man! His eyes wandered in vacancy, for they had lost their charm and their delight—his Elizabeth, his more than daughter, whom he doted on with all that affection which a man feels, who in the decline of life, having few affections, clings more earnestly to those that remain.

For they had called me mad, and during many months, as I understood, a solitary cell had been my habitation.

Liberty, however, had been a useless gift to me, had I not, as I awakened to reason, at the same time awakened to revenge.

"You are mistaken," said he.

"Man," I cried, "how ignorant art thou in thy pride of wisdom! Cease; you know not what it is you say."

And now my wanderings began which are to cease but with life. How I have lived I hardly know; many times have I stretched my failing limbs upon the sandy plain and prayed for death.But revenge kept me alive; I dared not die and leave my adversary in being.

When I quitted Geneva my first labour was to gain some clue by which I might trace the steps of my fiendish enemy. But my plan was unsettled, and I wandered many hours round the confines of the town, uncertain what path I should pursue. As night approached I found myself at the entrance of the cemetery where William, Elizabeth, and my father reposed.

I was answered through the stillness of night by a loud and fiendish laugh.

I pursued him, and for many months this has been my task.

Amidst the wilds of Tartary and Russia, although he still evaded me, I have ever followed in his track. The snows descended on my head, and I saw the print of his huge step on the white plain.

O blessed sleep! During the day I was sustained and inspirited by the hope of night, for in sleep I saw my friends, my wife, and my beloved country; again I saw the benevolent countenance of my father, heard the silver tones of my Elizabeth's voice, and beheld Clerval enjoying health and youth. What agonizing fondness did I feel for them! What his feelings were whom I pursued I cannot know. "

The rivers were covered with ice, and no fish could be procured; and thus I was cut off from my chief article of maintenance.

With new courage, therefore, I pressed on, and in two days arrived at a wretched hamlet on the seashore. A gigantic monster, they said, had arrived the night before, armed with a gun and many pistols, putting to flight the inhabitants of a solitary cottage through fear of his terrific appearance.

With what a burning gush did hope revisit my heart!

I pressed on, but in vain. In this manner many appalling hours passed; several of my dogs died, and I myself was about to sink under the accumulation of distress when I saw your vessel riding at anchor and holding forth to me hopes of succour and life. I hoped to induce you to grant me a boat with which I could pursue my enemy.But your direction was northwards.

If I do, swear to me, Walton, that he shall not escape, that you will seek him and satisfy my vengeance in his death. No; I am not so selfish.His soul is as hellish as his form, full of treachery and fiend-like malice. Hear him not; call on the names of William, Justine, Clerval, Elizabeth, my father, and of the wretched Victor, and thrust your sword into his heart.

Such a monster has, then, really existence! Sometimes I endeavoured to gain from Frankenstein the particulars of his creature's formation, but on this point he was impenetrable.

My thoughts and every feeling of my soul have been drunk up by the interest for my guest which this tale and his own elevated and gentle manners have created.

Our conversations are not always confined to his own history and misfortunes. What a glorious creature must he have been in the days of his prosperity, when he is thus noble and godlike in ruin! He seems to feel his own worth and the greatness of his fall.

Behold, on these desert seas I have found such a one, but I fear I have gained him only to know his value and lose him. I would reconcile him to life, but he repulses the idea.

If we are lost, my mad schemes are the cause.

Heaven bless you and make you so!

Frankenstein has daily declined in health; a feverish fire still glimmers in his eyes, but he is exhausted, and when suddenly roused to any exertion, he speedily sinks again into apparent lifelessness.

I mentioned in my last letter the fears I entertained of a mutiny. This morning, as I sat watching the wan countenance of my friend—his eyes half closed and his limbs hanging listlessly—I was roused by half a dozen of the sailors, who demanded admission into the cabin.

This speech troubled me. I had not despaired, nor had I yet conceived the idea of returning if set free. I hesitated before I answered, when Frankenstein, who had at first been silent, and indeed appeared hardly to have force enough to attend, now roused himself; his eyes sparkled, and his cheeks flushed with momentary vigour.

The die is cast; I have consented to return if we are not destroyed.

It is past; I am returning to England.

"They shout," I said, "because they will soon return to England."

"Alas! Yes; I cannot withstand their demands. I cannot lead them unwillingly to danger, and I must return."

At length he opened his eyes; he breathed with difficulty and was unable to speak. In the meantime he told me that my friend had certainly not many hours to live.

His sentence was pronounced, and I could only grieve and be patient. In a fit of enthusiastic madness I created a rational creature and was bound towards him to assure, as far as was in my power, his happiness and well-being.

My duties towards the beings of my own species had greater claims to my attention because they included a greater proportion of happiness or misery. The task of his destruction was mine, but I have failed.

I dare not ask you to do what I think right, for I may still be misled by passion.

His voice became fainter as he spoke, and at length, exhausted by his effort, he sank into silence.

My tears flow; my mind is overshadowed by a cloud of disappointment. But I journey towards England, and I may there find consolation.

I am interrupted. I must arise and examine.Good night, my sister.

what a scene has just taken place! I am yet dizzy with the remembrance of it. Never did I behold a vision so horrible as his face, of such loathsome yet appalling hideousness. I called on him to stay.

I approached this tremendous being; I dared not again raise my eyes to his face, there was something so scaring and unearthly in his ugliness.At length I gathered resolution to address him in a pause of the tempest of his passion.

I was at first touched by the expressions of his misery; yet, when I called to mind what Frankenstein had said of his powers of eloquence and persuasion, and when I again cast my eyes on the lifeless form of my friend, indignation was rekindled within me. "Wretch!" I said.

Yet such must be the impression conveyed to you by what appears to be the purport of my actions. Yet I seek not a fellow feeling in my misery. No sympathy may I ever find. I was nourished with high thoughts of honour and devotion. No guilt, no mischief, no malignity, no misery, can be found comparable to mine. Yet even that enemy of God and man had friends and associates in his desolation; I am alone.

For while I destroyed his hopes, I did not satisfy my own desires. They were forever ardent and craving; still I desired love and fellowship, and I was still spurned.

Fear not that I shall be the instrument of future mischief. My work is nearly complete. I shall die.

I leave you, and in you the last of humankind whom these eyes will ever behold.

Made in the USA
Coppell, TX
11 November 2024

40065265R00020